An A to Z of Pirates

Written by Caroline Stills

Illustrated by Heath McKenzie

LITTLE HARE
www.littleharebooks.com

A

is for **adventure**
on an **azure**-coloured sea.
Hoist the **anchor**, maties,
'tis a pirate's life for me.

B
is for **buccaneer**
(another pirate name).
Plundering for **booty**
is a **buccaneering** aim.

C

is for the **captain**.
Her **crew** is **cruel** and strong.
With treasure map
and **compass**,
she will never steer us wrong.

D

is for **duffle**,
a pirate's travel bag.
Inside are **deadly daggers**,
gold **doubloons**
and pirate flag.

E

is for **eye patch**,
to cover up a gash
made by cutthroat **enemies**
out to steal our cache.

F

is for **fearless**;
we bravely **face** our **foe**.
We love to pillage booty
wherever we may go.

PROPERTY OF THE FOE

G

is for **galleon**,
filled with jewels and **gold**.
Pearls and coins
and priceless **gems**
all **gleaming** in the hold.

H
is for **hunting**
for gold and buried treasure.
Ship ahoy, me **hearties**!
We'll plunder at our leisure.

TREASURE
IS MOST
CERTAINLY
NOT
HERE!!

NOT HERE!!!

INK

I
is for **island**,
where half our loot is hidden.
We know exactly where it is.
To tell *you* is forbidden!

J
is for **Jolly Roger**,
a flag with skull and bone.
Look, each one is different,
its owner clearly shown.

K

is for **kidnap**—
but do not be afraid.
We will always
bring you home…
once the ransom has been paid.

L

is for **landlubbers**,
who **live** upon the **land**.
But we prefer the ocean,
to a **life** that's dull
and planned.

M
is for **maroon**.
Dump the captain
on the shore.
It's a pirate **mutiny**—
'Don't want you any **more**!'

N

is for **navigation**
through unknown foreign seas.
Here's a chart,
so watch the stars
and sail the waves with ease.

O

is for **overboard**;
don't break the pirate code.
We make the traitors
walk the plank
to lighten up the load.

P

is for **parrot**,
the **pet** of the first mate.
It's **perched** upon
his shoulder
squawking '**pieces** of eight'.

Q

is for **quarterdeck,**
where Cook doles out our food:
pickled eggs and salted beef
or maybe fish that's stewed.

R

is for a tot of **rum**,
our favourite pirate drink.
But don't gulp down
too much at once,
or it might make you sink.

S

is for **shanty**,
a **sailor's** rhyming **song**.
It cheers us up
while trimming **sails**
and toiling all day long.

T

is for **treasure**,
on a **torn** and **tattered** map.
We'll have to search
the spot with care,
as sometimes there's a **trap**.

U

is for **ugly**,
untidy and **unclean**.
We think that baths
and washing
are a **useless** old routine.

V

is for **vessel**,
which we board
and then attack.
We take whatever we can find
and never give it back.

W

is for **weapons**,
like cutlasses and hooks.
Our **wooden** legs
don't hold us back,
we're toughened pirate crooks!

X

marks the spot, lads,
where treasure can be found.
Take your spades
and dig down deep:
it's buried underground.

Y

is the wide blue **yonder**,
with oceans to explore.
We **yearn** for new adventures
and a far-off foreign shore.

Z

is for **zephyr**,
a soft and gentle breeze.
Farewell, my friends,
we must depart
to sail the seven seas.

Did you find all of these objects in the pictures?

A
Aardvark
Abacus
Accordion
Aces
Acorns
Aeroplane (paper)
Alligator
Anchor
Angel
Antelope
Ants
Ape
Apple
Arrows
Astronaut
Axe

B
Balls
Barnacles
Barrel
Baseball bat
Bats
Bear
Bee
Bells
Belt
Bicycle
Bone
Boot
Bottle
Bow
Bubbles
Bucket
Buffalo

C
Candles
Candy cane
Cannon
Carrot
Cat
Caterpillar
Cauldron
Chains
Chocolate cake
Clocks
Clown
Cobra
Cockroach
Coffee
Cog
Compass
Corn
Cow
Crabs
Crate
Crayon
Crocodile
Crown
Cup
Cushions

D
Daggers
Dandelion
Darts
Diamond
Dice
Dinosaur
Doctor
Dog
Doll
Dominoes
Doorknob
Doughnuts
Dove
Dragon
Drill
Drum
Duck
Duffle bag
Dynamite

E
Eagle
Earphones
Eggs
Electric eel
Elephant
Elf
Eye patches

F
Fairy
Fan
Feather
Fire
Fireworks
Fish
Flies
Flowers
Flute
Fox
French fries
Frog
Frying pan

G
Galleon
Garden gnome
Gems
Ghost
Gift
Giraffe
Glasses
Glockenspiel
Gloves
Glue
Goat
Goggles
Gold
Goldfish
Gorilla
Grapes
Grass
Guitar

H
Hacksaw
Hairbrush
Halo
Hamburger
Hammer
Handbag
Hare
Harp
Hats
Hay
Heart
Hippopotamus
Hockey stick
Holly
Honey
Hook
Horse
Hotdog
Hot-water bottle

I
Iceblock (ice lolly)
Ice-cream
Icicles
Igloo
Iguana
Ink
Invisible man
Iron
Ivy

J
Jack-o'-lantern
Jaguar
Jam
Jelly beans
Jellyfish
Jester
Jigsaw puzzle
Jolly Roger
Judge
Jug
Juggling balls
Juice

K
Kangaroo
Keys
Kilt
Kite
Knife
Knight
Knitting

L

Ladder
Ladle
Ladybirds
Lamb
Lamp
Lamppost
Lantern
Lavender
Leaves
Lemons
Letter
Licorice
Licorice allsorts
Light
Lime
Lion
Loaf
Log
Lollipop

M

Mace
Mailbox
Mask
Maze
Melon
Mermaid
Mice
Microphone
Milk
Mirror
Money
Monkey
Moon
Mop
Moth
Moustache
Musical notes

N

Nails
Needle
Nest
Net
Newspaper
Ninja
Noodles
Nun
Nunchaku
Nutcracker
Nuts

O

Octopus
Onions
Oranges
Orangutan
Ostrich
Oven
Owl

P

Panda
Paper
Parrots
Pelican
Pencil
Penguin
Piano
Pie
Pizza
Poison
Polar bear
Pretzel
Pumpkin

Q

Quail
Queen
Question mark
Quilt

R

Rabbit
Raccoon
Racquet
Rat
Ribbon
Robber
Robot
Rocket
Rocking chair
Rocks
Rolling pin
Rooster
Rope

S

Sails
Sand
Sandwich
Saucepan
Sausage
Saxophone
Scarf
Sea
Seagulls
Seal
Shark's fin
Shell
Ship
Skeleton
Smoke
Snail
Snake
Soccer ball
Sock
Spider
Spoon
Squid
Star
Strawberries
Swing
Sword

T

Table
Tambourine
Tea
Teacup
Teapot
Tears
Television
Tennis ball
Tennis racquet
Thermometer
Thimble
Tiger
Tortoise
Train
Trap
Tree
Trophy

U

UFO
Ukulele
Umbrella
Underwear
Unicorn
Unicycle

V

Vacuum cleaner
Vampire
Vase
Vegetables
Viking's hat
Violin
Volcano
Vulture

W

Waiter
Walrus
Wardrobe
Wasp
Watch
Water
Watermelon
Weasel
Whale
Whip
Window
Witch's hat
Wolf
Worm

X

X-ray
Xylophone

Y

Yacht
Yak
Yoyo

Z

Zebra
Zeppelin
Zigzag
Zip
Zoo
Zucchini (courgette)

Glossary

Azure
a sky-blue colour

Booty
stolen goods taken from
an enemy

Buccaneer
a pirate

Cache
a store of hidden treasure

Cutlass
a short, heavy, slightly
curved sword, formerly
used especially at sea

Doubloon
a former Spanish gold coin

First mate
the next person in command
after the captain

Foe
an enemy

Galleon
a kind of large sailing ship

Jolly Roger
the pirate flag

Landlubber
someone who has never
been to sea

Loot
stolen goods

Maroon
to put someone ashore
and leave them behind
on a desert island

Mutiny
a revolt or rebellion by sailors
against their captain

Pillage
to rob or steal

Plunder
the same as pillage

Quarterdeck
an upper deck on a sailing ship

Ransom
the price paid or demanded
in exchange for a kidnapped
person

Shanty
a sailor's song, sung in rhythm
to work

Zephyr
a soft, mild breeze